No Private Life

NO
PRIVATE
LIFE

Michelle Boisseau

Vanderbilt University Press

Nashville, Tennessee
1990

Acknowledgments

Grateful acknowledgment is made to the editors of the following publications where some of these poems first appeared, sometimes in another form:

Anthology of Winners, 1985, Chester H. Jones Foundation: "In Her Parachute-Silk Wedding Gown"
California Quarterly: "Your Nightmares"
Cincinnati Poetry Review: "The Melancholia of Pleasure"
Crazyhorse: "The Night of the Breaking Glass," "Snorkeling," "Eurydice"
Georgia Review: "Tennyson Under the Yews," "Eavesdropping"
Missouri Review: "Pinwheel," "Under My Breath"
New England Review and Breadloaf Quarterly: "The Gloss Avenue Ghost"
The Ohio Review: "Equations," "A Marriage"
The Pikeville Review: "In the Mazy Gardens of the Ruined Hotel," "Charity Peaches"
Poetry: "Arbor Day," "Counting," "Mental Hospital Graveyard," "Partial Eclipse," "We Return to a Plain Sense of Things"
River Styx: "Persephone"
Seneca Review: "The Visible Man"
Telescope: "Inward, from the Air"

Some of these poems appeared in *East of the Sun and West of the Moon,* Stanley Hanks Chapbook Number Three, 1989, St. Louis Poetry Center.

With love and gratitude to Susan Prospere for her help and encouragement during the writing of much of this book. Thanks also to Bill Olsen, Nancy Eimers, and Jeff Greene.

Boisseau, Michelle, 1955–
    No private life / Michelle Boisseau.
        p. cm.
    ISBN 0-8265-1239-9
    I. Title
    PS3552.O555N6 1990
    811.54–dc20

                                                            89-77766
                                                                CIP

for my family
for Tom Stroik

Contents

"but there is no private life which has not been determined by a wider public life, from the time when the primeval milkmaid had to wander with the wanderings of her clan, because the cow she milked was one of a herd which had made the pastures bare."

—*George Eliot*

I

In Her Parachute-Silk Wedding Gown

She stands at the top of the aisle
as on a wing. The white paper
carpet is cloud
spilled out. The pillbox hats

turned to her are the rows
of suburbs she falls into.
She is our mother,
or will be, and any of us

stumbling upon this scene
from the next generation, would fail
to notice what makes even her
tremble, with her silver

screen notions of marriage—
where all husbands scold
to hide their good natures, and wives
are passionately loyal.

Her groom, after all, is just a boy
home from the war,
his only trophy, the parachute
she's made into her dress. It's a world

of appetites, she knows
all too well, waiting there
watching the flowers
bob in her hands, dizzying.

Despite herself, she's not thinking:
Go slowly, pace it,
a queen attended to court,
Bette Davis. Nor of the $20 bill

her mother safety-
pinned to her underpants.
But: My God,
a room full of men, looking,

each will ask me to dance—
your hand tingles
when you touch their close-
clipped heads. And the men,

nudged to turn around
and watch the bride descend,
see a fellow parachutist
as they all drift

behind enemy lines,
stomachs turning over as they fall
into the horizon, into the ring
of small brilliant explosions.

East of the Sun and West of the Moon

At first they seem quaint, set
among the outrageous props of another era,
their clothes merely costumes: Who can expect
true feeling from picture hats and plus fours?
Bending over them, bemused as the powers
in fairy tales, we breathe clouds—
like the North Wind—across the acetate,
across the generations of photographs.

But looking closer we lose them
like the sense of a new house—you wake up
that first night of the move to the floorboards
protesting your intrusion, and you walk them,
snapping on lights to wrest the rooms back
from the old owners who wiped their sleeves
on the windows, and deep in the pantry
that smells of wintergreen and witch hazel
left a jar of carriage bolts,
the exotic label of the commonplace.

Doughboy hat pulled over one eye—
in imitation of Garbo?—
our grandmother poses in her fiancé's uniform.
What to make of the grin, aimed
at the man fooling with the box camera?
Discovering, a week before the wedding,
how well she fit him?
Or teasing the returned soldier
with the way her breasts and hips strain
against the fabric of his clothes?
By the time we knew her, she'd folded herself up
like a sachet in a drawer, the guise
of a widow balancing a tray
of bone china, her body, through the chill fog.
The backdrop is foliage, full summer.
He arranged for a few spears of iris beside her,
no rooftops—no one else in the world
but her with the blank sky above her head.

In the Alms Hotel a bursting
flash startles the man and woman
whispering in the foyer.
The familiar shape of her lipsticked mouth,
his horn-rims—they're our parents,
but how much younger they are
than we who brush the dust from the page.
How sure they seem of their fine muscles—
his hand brought up as if he meant only
to protect her, the way she holds herself
under the gray bell of her dress,
its sheen like a woodland pool
where the lost one stops and drinks
and goes on, boots ringing
against the gathering ice.
They gave it all to us:
from silver to kodachrome this awful ease
of comparison. Their aged faces
lay always beneath the young
as if experience were only immersion,
a few moments rocked in the shallow waters
of the developing dish.

Standing together on the carpet,
the scalloped pattern like a tamed sea
at their feet—why should they care
how little we'll know them? When we have slipped
into the coming frailty, some other
generation will puzzle over us,
the small ceremony in the city gardens.
Our antique clothes whip about us
as we try to spray the newlyweds with rice
only to have the wind send it back,
seeding our hair, dropping like sleet.
into our plastic glasses.

Mental Hospital Graveyard

You might become sentimental over that starry atmosphere
that comes to so little. As you might over apples
shaded out by maples, or over the failure
of a brother who had such promise.
The rest of the farm was long ago subdivided,
but few living there know the orchard. In spring
the boughs hang like thousands of shredded shirts
left on a line through winter. In fall

there's hardly a bushel of apples to pick.
Where wisteria blooms across barbed wire,
the grounds begin. You've got to remember: gargoyles
and gardens clipped into clubs and hearts,
an architecture for people who think madness
a Rossetti romance. I was cutting through
when I ran across them. They're neat as Arlington graves—
you'd have noticed once—

but only numbered, up to twenty. Then down the rows
the numbers start over. The woman who took a razor
to her clothes after the Millfield mine
collapsed like a rotten floor, her husband inside,
could be mistaken for the soupy-eyed son
of Ruthie McAllister, raped by her uncle, or confused
with any number of those brought in from seven counties.
There's no use pitying those under numbered stones—

the retarded were rarely named anyway and the insane died
into other selves. And why blame the families?
Who'd want to drive all day from Gallipolis
or Letart Falls to see the brother
who couldn't know you? The dying farm's enough worry.
We have to leave room for other grief.
Supper time they must have still mimicked the brother's
old wisecracking ways. After the bad luck wore off

they probably named a son after him.
You can understand that, can't you? You used to
tease grandma when she went senile, pocketed the tip
she left at the dinner table. But you hushed me
when I laughed over it later. I've had to learn
certain signs—your eyes dilating
as you spin from the wheel, accusing me
of consorting with roadside trees and trucks.

I wish the hills roads didn't twist on themselves
and for once I could see as you do well enough
to bring you back whole into the long light
of these tall windows. I didn't spread branches
of blossom across the graves. I carried them
down the wide drive and home.
There, as frail flowers will,
they shed a simple cloth onto the table.

Fall on Your Knees, O Hear the Angel Voices

Only adolescents can ride untouched
through this battlefield. In our crimson capes
we hope to cut the figure of benefactress
come in velvet from carriage and castle gloom.
A flood, lavish down the bus steps, into
the antiseptic hall, we roll in among the old folks
like a red tide, mouthing Os. Oceans
of O Tannenbaum, O Little Town of Bethlehem,
O Holy Night wash over the tiny ones
sinking in wheelchairs, clutching walkers,
and floundering in goofy confusions. Armored
with sex as though we had willed to rise from us
the breasts and mysterious hair, we offer ourselves
as munificent examples: if only the old
could get a good look at us, they'd give up
their bad habits, their clicking joints;
they'd *will* themselves out of their chairs
to applaud and admire us. First we sing to them,
then we pat and smile at them like Glenda
to Dorothy; we present them with pink bottled
bubble bath, candy canes to suck, brooches
made from midget pine cones. They rattle
the tissue paper and hang the ribbons
from their necks. A dozen times I've remembered this—
endless carols, their weird laughter, the scrawny
tree decked in chains—but only now have I looked
off in the corner. Wrapped up beside a window
cratered with frost, a radiator hissing and heaving,
she shrugs me off like a child refusing to take
her medicine. I touch her, she flinches:
after all these years she still won't look at me
even when I tear her gift open—a plastic comb
in a plastic sleeve—and test how true
its strong blunt teeth ring out against my nail.

Eavesdropping

It was Mrs. Garvin, the doctor's wife,
who told my mother, Well if you're that broke
put the kids up for adoption.
Out under the porch light that summer
we slapped at mosquitoes and invented
our brave escape—luminous sheets
knotted out the window
were the lines of a highway down the house.
We would know the way,
like ingenious animals, to go
quietly toward the river,
but we could imagine no further
than the shacks on stilts
shivering the water,
the Kentucky hills on the other side.
Denise, the youngest, took to sleepwalking,
wading room to room for the place
one of us—curled up in a bed's corner—
might have left her. I'd wake
with her face pressed against my back,
her hands reining the edges of my nightgown.
I didn't tuck her into my shoulder
but loosened her fingers and led her
back to her own bed, her fear
already seeping into me like water
or like the light spilling
‐from the milk truck
as it backfired down the street.

Under My Breath

1

It weighs less and less—
that image of you drunk in the doorway
filling the room with the sour smell
of the undigested. My sisters have suddenly
gone quiet, their bodies dark knots in blankets.
I lean up on the pillow so you can see
only me—Maybe she's downstairs somewhere—
I tell you, breathing with her
to cover her sound. You joke how your zipper
got stuck so your shoes squeak
with urine. It is the night you throw
yourself against the front door until casing
and chain give way and the house
shakes after you: Tell your mother
she can't lock your father out.
In the morning you've been gone hours
when we sift through loose boards like flood victims.
The light from the hall leaks
over the shoulder you rub, as you spread
your hand toward me.

2

On a Sunday afternoon my brother and I hide
in the closet. You tell her you want
to start all over. We have already
kicked shoes out of place
and now press ourselves between dresses.
We will never talk about this
although he will hold me in his arms.
Years later she says you weren't drunk
but crazy. My brother's hair stands
straight up, the way it's cut.
When you leave, we walk out on the porch,
look up the street, look down.

3

You wink at the man by the tent flap,
wave your hand like the snake charmer and lead
your children past the cages rocking
with lions, past the white horse and the lady
who rides bareback. We hurry after
your coattails. At my mother's house
a photograph shows how you picked me
off the sawdust, my legs dangling
over your crooked arm,
how I am so small when you hold me
high up near the heads of the elephants.

Equations

A.

The garden shovel turns up
a mole's nest. The young are the pink
and dirt-clottled fingers of a child
who has dug all morning in the cold spring mud.
Their paddle feet, smaller than fingernails,
stroke the crumbs of soil
with the absorption of long–distance swimmers.
While I hold the dog back—he's gone vivid
with the smell—I cup
one soft body. It keeps swimming
for that close dark that touches
completely, the dark only breathers like these
belong to. For a moment the sun comes out.
The leaf buds shake their shadows
across the dirty tools. Distracted
by how the garden looks, I'm too late
to stop the dog. And the baby mole
still swimming in my hand for home
is the only one left.

B.

As children we believed in wishful thinking,
and our wishes were large
and simple as equations or a child's ideas
of marriage. Father played along,
showing up for his visits
with the summer afternoon pocketed with plans.
At the marina upriver, for instance,
the lounge, dark and cold with air conditioning,
was strung with anchors and life preservers
to protect a childish sense
of the nautical. Facing the bar
where father waited, portholes
looked into the deep end of the pool
that was sunk in the clubhouse ceiling.
From the roof we saw the muddy river

curving low in its banks, heard the knocking
at the docks. In the chlorine water
the dark windows shone
like dropped coins. We dove for them.
We held our breath and held
onto the porthole rims. It didn't matter
that we saw only amber lights glinting
and something white moving pendulously.
He waved. We gripped the rims and held
our bodies straight and open as spoons.

Preparing for the Funeral

The sacristan admires the smooth blond
wood of his broom as he sweeps to the gutter
the orangey wings and glumped bodies: in the trees

still a few pathetic cries—sexsexsex—
17 years of sucking roots, sub-terra,
only to flit briefly in the hivey dark of leaves.

Silently down the aisle's gloom we scuff—
not out of respect but reluctance—toward the loud
blooms, laid in loose chains across the offering

that they've wheeled before the shushed altar.
Inside their dark suits, the ushers
fidget and sweat. A row of women bending

hat brims over their eyes. A boy in lustrous
black shoes patrols the periphery,
clicking windows shut with a long pole.

Flicker in the vestibule, white vestments:
who is coming to mutter ceremony
beyond the polished rail? Whose hands

will they shut around a rosary? O my sister
lay your head in the cup of my shoulder,
the smell of your hair more familiar than all others.

Let's twist our fingers together like rope
so neither can be taken, or both at once,
for we could not bear it—seeing
the other under that confusion of flowers.

15

The Melancholia of Pleasure

I carry mine slung on the hip.
Susan cradles hers low in front, full-bellied,
up the walk to Nancy's in small, imperial steps.

No children of our own, we're resolved
to mark the occasion anyway, to take knives
to the essential, cut and scrape
the pumpkins' jewelry of seeds. The slippery
membranes slide from our grasp as we rip
the casings clean, golden bodies
piling in the porcelain bowl.

Over western fences, the autumnal light
retreats like a well-traveled suitcase—folded inside
lies the scarlet of the trees. Children flood
their rooms with light—the better to see
as they scissor into paper sacks
a place to breathe.

At last we dip matches into the fleshy caverns.
The candles sputter and stand,
obedient subjects. Plumping up pillows
and settling down with tea and cake, we admire
the people we've made, the eyes
that float like keyholes in a darkened room,
the artifice. Braids of smoke
unwind from one head's jagged seam

as we take deep draughts and lick the icing
from our fingers. At doors where wings beat
the porch light into tatters, the children appear,
tugging at their obvious disguises.

Arbor Day

Above the house, the topmost branches reel
and shudder in mimicry of how the maples
trembled when they were saplings
and children carried them here from school
like staffs of office. The house creaks tonight

with the lives of all its owners
as though no one ever moved away or grew up
into forgetting. The children wake
with the storm. Through streaking windows
lightning casts quick shadows in the hall

where the children gather. Their talk is the sighing
of stairs, the shifting weight of old furniture.
It's small wonder then
that the new owner passes them by
as he comes down to check the doors and look out

on the lawn where leaves float
in battered puddles. Someone cut a row
into the shin-high grass then left
the push mower stopped like an idea
in mid-sentence. The flashing singles out

the blades, the wind rocks
the handle as if to finish the chore.
By dawn each shadow has climbed back
through the trees. The maples described a circle
around the one that has fallen.

II

Counting

After a while, remembering the men you loved
is like counting stars.
From the arbitrary constellations
you pick out those the brightest. Then the others,
dimmer and dimmer until you can't tell
if they're real or only reflections
from your eyes watering with the strain.
The body's memory is a poor thing. Ask the adopted child
who falls asleep against any steady heart,
to a lullaby in any language.
Between my first lover who was thin
and my second who was warm and nostalgic,
my arms remember little. Though, yes,
there was one who had that sweet smell in his skin
of a child who still drinks nothing
but milk. A milk ladled out
by the Big and Little Dippers. If you look up
long enough into the night sky,
it becomes surer of itself and you less sure
whether you're lying on the lawn, skirt tucked
against mosquitoes, a cigarette
about to burn your fingers,
or if you're falling, and the sky
is a net that can't catch you
since, like everyone else, you are water
nothing can stop. So you lie on your bed,
all night staring at the cracks
in the ceiling, terrified of falling through.

Pinwheel

It's like a life (I could say)
one day's small ambitions blur
into the next, most of the edges wheel off
in the gewgaw's turning. Until it stops.
Only then can the children left make out
the parts from the whole, the pointed petals
that their breath can't start.
I'd say that and you'd be unimpressed.
You already know my love for the devotional
poetry of the seventeenth century.
Those three nights and days running last fall,
drifting through insomnia with the choices
in our lives, I filled the hours
with all the poems of George Herbert,
those golden staircases winding
and winding up. But when I finished, I pitied
the dead man, his chapels moldering
under heaps of ivy and sunflowers.
When I got into bed, you were waking, the sky
just going to that backwards blue
of the south's humid autumns.
We called ourselves sentries in recognition
of harm's way. You pulled the damp sheets
up to my chin: sleep now.
And sometimes I did. This is the cheapest
pinwheel I've ever seen.
The orange plastic clip of its nose
clashes with the red-silver,
blue-gold petals, sea-green handle—
a child's love of detail
for the sake of detail. It's by a kind of choice
we call circumstance that we're childless.
So we let the ideas about parents
and children blur a little. When I found this
at the drugstore, crammed in a vase of spinning toys,
I knew you'd let me give it to you.

Snorkeling

The shore houses are Victorians
for those who wander out too far.
I've listened hard to you and still don't know
what I'm doing: how to blow the water out
that keeps choking me, how to stay calm
despite the fish, long as my forearm,
flickering in this prehistoric light
that washes you and sea urchin
and starfish with pale, suspended

particles—disintegrated stars
no human ever looked on.
Your childhood wet suit is too big on me.
The water rushes in cold as recognition
of my own failings. Even the sea prairie,
articulating itself with easy rolling,
reminds me I overestimate myself.
And you've never looked so concerned
when I finally give it up

and crawl to shore on mussel edges,
cutting my numb hands, sliding
with my flippered feet
on the trailing beards. By the time the sun
unshivers me, I'm sun- and wind-burnt
and you come swimming out. In one hand
you hold the spear gun.
On its shaft a fish is flapping.
Curling up, in the other, a palm-sized star.

Your Nightmares

It's the least duty of insomnia.
Your breath quickens you—

I put my book on its face
and bend over you as you rush

into the nightmare.
I hold back but the dream worsens,

so I touch my two fingers
to your back, down the spine

like the feet escaping
on the fantastic stair.

I hate to invade the private course
of events, my arm coming down

as if from the sky—
a long shadow thrown

across the countryside
where the workers look up

from their threshing and know
terror. But now you've begun

breathing slowly—the shadow has
dropped into pieces

which your villagers fashion into glorious windows.
I am glad to have taken you out of that country.

Here the night goes on as before: the gods
ride around in the muttering

clouds, glance down
from their beds and don't interfere.

Behind Clinch Mountain

Upright, rusted, ridiculous, it stands
opened and aching with a load
of piled snow—the ironing board someone
set up in the middle of the clearing and left.
I was holding my breath to be light enough
to walk on top the frozen snow when the fallen trees,
sheeted like bodies in a bed, reminded me
of our long–distance argument last night,
and the snow collapsed beneath me like the floor
of a weak conviction. And then I saw it—
anachronism, rusted legs so deep
in the snow it could be a stretcher
or that narrow cot we tried and broke to bits.
Did someone dump it—a favorite sport around here—
to watch it wind and bounce down a hillside
and end with its face in a creek, tended
only by the sympathetic shapes of trillium leaves?
And later another, a woman perhaps
thinking of packing up the kids and walking out,
rescued it and dragged it along with her
so she could practice moving, and opened it
to see a household out of doors. Then one fall,
a boy found it and lit the candle stub he carried—
here the wax fell into a pool—
and made sandwiches from the bread and sliced meat
he'd stolen in town. After eating, slowly,
watching the leaves spill into the dim spaces
and not fill them and keep on falling,
he decided to go back and sleep
in his own bed again, to wake to the blue and yellow
pennants of his childhood. With my forearm
I push off all the snow and lie down,
one foot on the ground to carry off my weight.
Each time now, your voice on the phone
becomes like words said over and over
until they don't mean "cup" or "spoon" anymore
but float off—snow borne from branches—
all those years together flitting
between me and a sky so blue
it hurts to look long at it.

Partial Eclipse

A scrap of white through dense
hedges—her hair or blouse. Day or night
when you pass the porch, she sits between two pillars
of paperbacks. At her left hand
those unread, at her right the pile mounts
through summer until one slides off
into the brown needles. The glum face

on the cover might mean something
as the birds mean something more
than you are sick of them,
how they fly at the slightest noise,
your lover who cannot keep his mind on you.

Who are you fooling with this fiction?

She is you, if anyone, since you made her up
out of this morning
of mere disappointment in him—which means
"no point at all"—except in the partial eclipse
that drops hooks and horns
from leaf shadow, the only spectacle
you're supposed to look at.

Stay in the deep shade of the porch.
The sun is harmful
because the eye trusts it and opens
and stays open even after the harm is done.

The Anniversary

Let's get this right.
First, that day was little different from others:
the argument between us like a torn bird
on a platter, the vague collapse of its parts
stuck to the cooled butter.

And second, all afternoon I'd watched you shedding the sea
off Napatree Point. The cormorants,
ticked by the invasion, unfolded from their aeries
like black newspapers. The book of my hands
lay open as I could not read it.

> But for you that afternoon
> was all irritations—
> the face mask leaked in strings of sea:
> you shot the spear gun into the rocks.
> When you swam in to straighten the shaft,
> I must have looked ridiculous, wedged
> into the water that pooled in your mask,
> and then my moodiness like a cloud of sand
> the tide rolled against you.

And last, on the way back—
didn't you drive?—
yes, you were glad to be intent on it—
the black mirror of Merritt Parkway,
the tunnel of traffic, no way you could turn to me
though you must have felt my eyes on you.
                                    But you're wrong,
I hoped for nothing from you. I'd become fascinated
with the browned skin of your arm, sea salt
crystalizing in the golden hairs:

                        though I was so angry
I had to sit on my hands, I wanted to taste that salt,

take the blade of my tongue and travel
the length of you. For I could see the years
with me had left no mark on you.

We Return to a Plain Sense of Things

You will not answer his letters, flimsy blue
envelopes with continental postmarks—
flattened pods that sing
one note in the garden. Answer enough
in the golden world falling, wheels
spinning past the window and clicking
into place on the brown grass
as the blue foil of winter takes up
where the momentary splendor of leaves has failed.

He writes as though it were another life ago,
that summer you lay together in the rented bed
while the rowboat struck music
from the dock, now and then the plash
of a fish erupting like sudden knowledge.
Then the starry quiet continued
and he went on sleeping.
In the morning the elegant architecture
of swans glimpsed through the rushes.
How they fussed up the bank when you broke up
bread for them, silty black webs
gripping the stones, the sedge's teeth snaring
bits of their down. And if you were too slow
to empty your hands, they wrestled
the crusts from your palms.

And it is morning too in this new life—
another man leans up on the mounded pillows
and peels away the blankets
to take in all of you. His expression would say
you have come from nowhere. The avenues
throw down their camouflage and the town
reappears. The milkweed delivers
its last messages. Against the frost
you have carried in every flower—
chrysanthemums and asters
you let rot in the vase. Their hearts curl up
and litter the table, exposing the stub of pistil,
the corona of stamen. You may be wooed again,
but you will not be won.

Son et Lumière

A story told with lights flashed across the chateau,
with sound effects rumbling afterwards
through the flowers. A story we lost track of

as soon as it started though I wanted to lose myself
in its details. The guards' flashlights ushered
my friends and me into the crowded gardens

where mosquitoes cruised from ornamental moats
to hum in our ears. Two hundred yards away,
Chenonceaux, part castle, part bridge,

white stones arching across arches shifting
on the river Cher—long-legged birds, wings
lifted tip to tip. A portal jumped

under a searchlight, a medieval air
seeped from loudspeakers, and the narrator's French
launched into calm waters: we understood these

to serve as introduction, but we could make out
only a few random words, the thin
frame of the story, none of its furniture.

Remembering that summer now, I can't remember
the unhappy luggage I carried through Europe,
the summer five years of love ended. I go back

with a tourist's curiosity, a tourist's distance:
the tie is severed between how I felt
and what I did while I was feeling.

Without atmosphere there are no sounds,
but light sifts through every empty space,
thankfully, light but no heat.

The sound and light show at the chateau
got underway with a shower of red lights
strobing the river (a battle depicted?),

and then moments later, dragging behind
through the moist air like reluctant servants,
the sound effects: boom of cannon,

fife and drum. But by the time the sounds
reached us the story that the lights told
had gone on to other matters (repartee

of candles in the gallery) that didn't match
the urgent static of the chronicler,
the breaking glass, the crackling fire:

it was history as glamor, as roast swan
and brocade, grand passions grandly betrayed.
No cooks or weavers to that story, nor the itch of haying,

the buzz in the gutters—those elements
I used to nag him about, the history
he liked to overlook. The trouble is

we have only the one word, history,
though it has two habits. It means what happened—
an abstraction pure and uncertain as physics.

But also: the story we tell of what happened.
We live on the stretch between them
as we live between the unimpeded fact

of light and the muffled noise that attends
it on the ground. Still, I've wanted to float back there,
into the thick of it, the acre of petunias

throwing their scent into the air, to tell myself
how I'll come out of it, how that sad luggage
gets lost in time: first in light

that keeps going until it is the rice of stars,
then in sound where it becomes a story
I might tell myself to sleep.

Psyche

Turn away, now you have found him.
He sprawls on his mother's couch, eating
red Sicilian oranges. In the doorway his mother hugs
bandages for him to her breasts, purple veils
storming over her shoulders. She thinks she made him
up and now can rewrite him. Turn away,
scramble back down the hill, through the orchard, away,
before someone catches you misting the windows.
The end of the journey is blurry as the ends

of a rope, as the underside of apples beneath the ransacked
trees, as those soldiers lying face down
in the charred field, the wind coming up to fret
the fires sore again. All you wanted was to look
into his face as lovers do. It was always dark when he
came in to you, the hairs of his legs prickling
you awake, your hands, caught back in his, beating
feebly as leaves. Morning, only a pillow
wedged under your hip. His mother is unrolling

the bandages as she purses her lips to blow his hot wound
cool. Good enough for him. Turn away. When he entered you
you split open, a pod, oil oozing down your thighs. The brimming
lamp was heavy with doubt—that's why
you spilled it—not for his beauty. His mouth swollen
from kissing. Has he told her about that? Or how
mortally his groans seeped out afterwards?
And then he was gone, the house and gardens, like a bird
that left no trace beneath the trees. You wanted to see.

Eurydice

It isn't you he wants, but the getting you out.
Even before you can see him, you can tell
he's coming, feelingly along the slick walls
the way, up there, you told rain by the dank
quiver it dragged across a field or news by the lull
of a dumbstruck street. The smell of sunlight

drops like money from his clothes.
Foreign currency. What does he want with you?
The phosphorescence of this place slides off him
in blue ribbons. Enough light to see a page by
though not to read it. Rubbing your hands,
blowing sticky breath across your fingers,

he tilts his head to one side as if to tip you
into him, as if you were small enough
to fit in his pocket. Far in the glass
carapace of yourself, you remember him,
a subterranean coal you can feel no longer.
There is no more sadness here than heat.

Regret is a fine soft sand that floats
around bodies or clumps in corners like cotton
spilled from a ship and stumbling through a town.
It wasn't the songs he sang to you,
but the singing: his voice ripped
the air open, a gold knife in a red melon.

Too surprised at first to feel
the pain of such beauty, desire, desire
climbed out of the gleaming black seeds.
Did you learn your lesson? You know
he won't resist turning around. You know,
once he treads out of the limey dark,

he'll forget you for the songs in his head.
Why do you follow him then? Is it to watch him
emerge, the fringe of yellow closing
around his hair? Is it that in the mouth
of the cave you'll have time
to fill your lungs before going down?

Persephone

You feel drunk with gorgeousness, filled up
on foods he wouldn't touch—overripe pears
that dribble down your chin, cheeses
pungent as the warmth of animals,
and sour bread smeared with tomatoes and garlic.

Already you've caught yourself
eyeing the village boys. In from the fields
one takes his tunic to his sweaty brown face
(even his lips are sunburnt)
and then slowly to his neck: he knows
you're watching. If he leaves the shirt
hanging from the cart, you'll steal away
with it; what a heady pillow it would make.
All this jostling in the market, you've lost count
of how many strangers have touched you.
Your hands sticky with coins, your ears
ringing with the clamor of chickens.

Freckling your arms, the sunlight stamps out
your winter. But how you once admired him!
His body like a blade of frost.
His head lifted above his ledgers
like a moon in the caves: he knew the silvered
end of every story. And when he laughed
it seemed he could hear into the deepest passages
where white moss and salts grew into sculpture
and hidden waters ticked dimly as clocks.

Tonight why not take this boy
up the hillside with you? And as he sleeps,
a heavy leg flung over your hips,
you can look down on the village
where it is never truly quiet. A baby
cries to be nursed. In the granary mice chew
into a sack and a torrent of corn
rains over them. The face of an owl
glows in the rafters. But yours is brighter—
drenched with dew, you lie remorseless
as a river unraveling under the open sky.

Snow White and Rose Red

Before the man in the bear suit
huffed through the thigh-high snow
and rapped at their door like a broken shutter,
before he looped them in with stories, suspending
them, like trussed game, in his plots,
what did the sisters tell each other?
"The fire warms us, Rose Red"?
"The white stones of the swept hearth
cool us, Snow White"? Always,
always is. But then he came, his stories
so sad the shadows hummed in the corners
like feral things. Which was it—
a story of pleasure as when he took off the hide
or the pleasure of story—that made them sigh?

A Marriage

She can be two places at once—
at the sink, water
trailing up her arm as she lifts a plate.
(She must hurry before he comes home
like clockwork.) And out the window where pokeweed

flows up from the thicket—
the eyes draw the picture in
as if on thin threads then hang it in the head:
the black-purple bush
clamoring with bruised jays.
In spring it grew like a bride,

white berries on frail green stems,
then summer coursed
red into the thickened veins and purpled the fruit
which is poison to humans but delicious
to those black and blue birds. How beautiful they are
and noisy

like the girls she remembers at school.
They'd drop their books down a stairwell
just to show the likes of her
how many people listened. At the grocery, maybe she'll be
lifting limes into her basket one by one

and they come pressing toward her, their children
a wake behind them: "And your husband?
How's he?" as they look
her up and down.

Of all the girls in the high school gymnasium
why'd he pick her out?
She was sitting there so quiet,
fingering the stiff collar of a nosegay
someone had left on the folding chair seat
shining beside her.

If the eyes hang pictures,
the skin that feels is a house
and all the windows are lit in the middle of the night,
the guests gathering
for some news just arrived, good or bad.
Or only one person,

methodical, he searches the house,
room to room, flicking on lights, poking under beds
and into closets with a flashlight:
come out, come out now.

Charity Peaches

for Martie

After the storm quits the orchard,
rotten branches dangle from hinges of bark.
Here the orphans worked in summer to learn
the value of working for nothing—for the few pies
in soggy crust, for preserves that gathered dust
on the orphanage shelves then showed up
one breakfast, winter suns dolloped
into white saucers. Tonight, their bodies
rigid as candles in a window, two girls
have been watching. What with the thunder
that drove the younger into the bed of the older,
and the lightning that kept trying to get in
the last word, both are awake when a milky face
from a big coat, a woman it looks like,
wanders up the drive. She is the moon come out
to make the dark an orchard again.
She is a silver button. She is a needle
appearing and reappearing in the weave
of the low trees. She's come for me,
says the girl with thick glasses.
For me, the sad one who chews paper.
She disappears so long into a row they figure
she'll sleep there, brushing away the old pits,
pillowed on the roots. The girls bunch their pillows
against the window sill and doze off.
What wakes them up? The beaded glass
whines when they wipe it clear. There she is,
standing in the open, hair hanging down
her back like a wrinkled blanket. She looks
into the leafy cascade she's pulled down—
as if checking the part on a head—then fastens
something there, and there, and farther down the row.
So they argue, she's going to the woods.
No, see her through the leaves, moving
like the leaves? As it gets light,
they can't wait another minute
and boost each other out the laundry window,
pajamas darkening to the knees in the wet grasses.
Hanging by bits of cloth from the branches,
they decide, are locks of hair—red-gold,
a soft yarn between their fingers—
a trail that leads to the wire fence
where she cut off and tied the last scrap
before climbing over in her shining helmet.

In the Mazy Gardens of the Ruined Hotel

for Loretta

His mother's prickling laugh, the copper
voices of his aunts: they've gone somewhere
inside the high blooming corridors, shining hedges.
It's the sound of them forgetting him, the sound
of their talk just before he enters a room.
They've lost him—he meant to stay close,
but the bees were crossing overhead like shoestrings,
then plunging into the petals' pink quiet. A bee,
rowing around the furniture of flowers,
sounds like the time he fell from the raft
into the motel pool, into the whir

and chug of filtered water. With only the baby-sized oar
they'd given him, he churned himself around
until he became a dimple on the surface, trees
smearing past like glass around a caught bug.
He sank like a nickel, they said. A drowned fly
floated past, green jacket fuzz, purple
wings like tiny screens: When you die,
he thought, you see like flies.
In *National Geographic* once, two eyes filled
a page, rows of black squares—

his mother's metallic evening bag, they way it winks
from her arm when she kisses him goodnight.
And then the room goes dark, and their high shoes
tick on the walk, the applause
of their car starting up. They won't believe
a trapdoor opened under the drain or the water
hugging his head was jelly, the crushed cherries
his aunts stir in the pots. The flattened grass
where they just were standing, the three of them circled
around a match, is rising up blade by blade
like the hair on a cold arm catching the sun.

They're coming back now, calling his name,
tangling it in the long leaves, slipping
their voices among the motors of wind
and bees. Coming closer. So he must hurry.
The bees spill away in every direction
as he snaps off the flowers, so many loading his arms
some drop at his feet like loosed laundry,
and he piles them up on the grass, shapes the blooms
into a blurry body, the wet shadow you make
beside a pool, but pink—the color of the world
when they pull you from the depths,
cupped in their many hands.

The Gloss Avenue Ghost

Open a door or window upstairs, and downstairs
          papers drift to the floor.
Or a scarf hung on a doorknob fans its tassels
          as if to finger the air's disturbances.
This house always breathed like that—my wife called
          it sympathy, but I knew it
              as a drafty house. The lady who lives
here now wasn't wakened,
as I was, when her oldest boys inched up
          their window and shimmied down
              where an auto, taillights glowing,
rolled down the hill before its engine
          started up and took them away.
I try to watch after them
          as far as I can. The mother worries.
Nine children. The mother and her mother—just a shadow
            mumbling. And two fat orange cats
          that sleep in the windowsills—east, mornings,
          west, afternoons—and one shivering
bitch puppy, pregnant her first year,
          forgotten tonight outside.
              She ran barking after the boys,
but not fast enough, limped back
          and settled herself into a pile of leaves
          swept in a porch corner.

I was here first, but no matter.
I always did like the hours
          after a party—the world
          hushed like now, candles
putting themselves out in their own puddles,
          quiet like the night river, close in to shore.
            On the floor maybe a handkerchief
              dropped when a sweating girl
finally let herself go in the dance. Upstairs,
my wife asleep in the nursery, the nurse
          asleep in a chair.

This lady falls asleep
sitting up too, sometimes sleeps here
through the night, curling in
as it gets colder, until at dawn
she stomps her feet to wake them.
They hurt her like ungrateful children.
Now and then she'll start up and look straight through me
and around the room for balance
at the jackets and shoes with tongues loose
and newspapers, some twisted
into kindling then left
to unwind through the night,
or, one of her children comes down and shakes her
and pulls her arms.
We leave each other be—too many boats
in the middle of the river, too many
children in this house, three to a room
like cousins on holidays,
but these scramble against each other—
crabs in a bucket.
If you pilot the barges close along the banks
where the trees droop like velvet
to a theatre box,
and if you've lived with the river, like a wife or a house—
the wide shallow bends and sandbars
rising in the seasons—
you'll stay clear of the rest and wakeful
in courting the small danger. It floats
on the tongue like the last transparent
sliver of a lozenge.
My wife kept a bowl
of lemon drops like these and my head in her lap.
Lifting the sour sweet
past my lips, she talked me into more
than she ought, then let me drift off.

No one ever stays put in this house.
                    One now at the head of the stairs,
              head cocked, squinting and hearing
        a nervous leaf in the windy sills.
    The crowding makes some of them mopey. Yesterday
              I found one little girl squeezed
        in the old coal chute with a novel
                    and a flashlight.
        She put both down suddenly
and cried for a solid hour. And me there useless—
        a stranger at a small town funeral.
                    With my wife it was different.
        Her sadness grew on her
              like wild grapes. The vines can climb
                    from nowhere and up a river sycamore,
                    and the wide leaves spin
        a twilight in a summer noon.
Nothing pleased her then.
                    Twice a day, she dragged
              the furniture around as though some secret
                    clock signaled her.
        Late into the quiet
sometimes, I hear the echoes of the bureaus
              and wardrobes and divans scraping the floors,
                    years of drifting until a cliff face
                    caught the sound
        and sent it home. All sounds float back
sooner or later though no one hears
        or they arrive without warning.
                    The time I found her gasping
              against the bookcase, a trail of books
        spilling open as if trying to find a word
                    for her, she had pried
        all the ivories from the piano
                    and dropped them
        in the commode.
        Her mother's piano,
all that was left of England.
                    She scared the daylights
              out of the girls. When I finally came home,
        riding up, they flew to me,

44

pressed their faces against
                the haunches of the horse—
I had grown so large in my absence.
                But not large enough
        for them to remember—or want to—
                        how they came running. These children
            are bad mannered,
                but they don't pretend to forget.

Too many boats in the middle, and too many
                children riding this house, a boat
        so low in the water, the river
                laps in.
That load of goosedown from Illinois—
                        it was not
        the sailing in close
                (despite the lawyers),
                        it was our damned, worthless
            French boat—cracked in two.
            A blizzard in July.
That lazy flatboater (lawyer's nephew) following us
        for a river guide
                nearly drowned
    with feathers when he opened his mouth to curse us.
What's that dog
                going on about now? Maybe the boys
                        coming home or someone sleepless
                on Ridge Road.
                        Pitiful thing—
shaking on the step, barking
        with bits of leaf stuck to her.
                        The trees along the river
        grew feathers
                as though leaves were a momentary disguise
and one by one each tree
                would take wing
                        from the shattered boat
            and barges riding
                        up the sandbar,
one on top the next,
            the other boats spinning
                        around and over to avoid us.

45

One of the girls is running to shush the dog.
Barefoot on the porch,
a night like this. Muddy paw prints
up her nightgown.
My Nellie's age when they took her.
And is she carrying that little dog,
leaves and all, to bed with her?
If only all trouble could be soothed
with an embrace until you slept
under the weight of the wool.
She didn't get the door
shut tight. The grandmother,
hunches over here, door wide open,
dead of winter, calling the cats—
which are sleeping upstairs.
The girls hurry by as if they live
down the block.
Three days on trains
to see my girls in Grand Haven
and they just stood on the stoop, grimly
blinking to show no intention
of asking me in.
It was after the wreck
and the lawyers
she took them, that nothing
brother of hers insisting.
Bess was fat
in all the wrong places. And Nell
chewed her lip like a sentence
in German till my eyes stung.
I should have shaken the silliness from them.
They weren't mine anymore.
I was no one but the house's
which is only a house after all.
But then.
When I'd be down to Memphis or Louisville
and they still here, I'd lie awake
on my bed on the river—rocking above me
the lantern on a hook, in good weather
its handle clicking, a steady heart,

and I'd make the house up, pacing
                    the rooms in my head—
         the smell of turpentine
              in the cellar cupboard, the "Morning
                        Gloriouses," as we called them,
     climbing the screens. Nellie
         hopscotching up and down, down
                   and up the stairs, bouncing twice
                        for the music
     on the third last stair that always wheezed.
     And then I wasn't on the river
                        but with them because longing
              carries you home. She told me
some nights maybe she felt me here.
                   Maybe she did.

The lady's stretching awake now, complaining softly
                        over her stiff hands.
         Reaching into the cushions, frowning,
              she pulls out the blue ceramic horse
     I saw the children bury solemnly last evening.
The ugly chair will keep her shape
                   a little while, then give it up
         to the slow steady dawn. Holding herself
     carefully in half-sleep, she'll look over each bed,
              then for a few hours
                   lie on top her own.
The boys are back now
                   and almost all of us are asleep.

IV

The Visible Man

for Bartolomeo Martello

After the anesthesiologist
took you under, cupping your face
like a swim master teaching you
to swim backwards, did you swim back
to Campania?
At the inn halfway between villages
the tables are set.
Your aunts flick their petticoats
and talk softly beside the arbor.
Swinging from every tree along the road
are paper lanterns that signal
one another with the lightest breeze.
You walk beneath, peeling an orange, careful
to keep the rind whole.
When you can no longer tell
the lanterns from the village
or the faint music
from the tune you carry, you twist the peel
back into an orange
and throw it over your shoulder
for good luck in America.

When I was a child, we had a toy
with transparent skin called The Visible Man.
In surgery his organs snapped out
and we arranged them along the floor
according to whim—
as if the body's form were accidental.
Though of different colors and shapes,
the organs seemed the same.
None slid from your fingers
or bled at a touch. But if a part was gone—
the heart carried off for a Monopoly piece—
the man with see-through skin
looked awkward, someone with a missing tooth
caught before the camera.
Later my mother told me about Michelangelo,
how he once lifted the intestines
out of a cadaver, and lifted them out,

yards and yards
kept unfolding, a roadmap
that never folded the same again.

I am so happy you've come back to us.
The heart is heavy,
and the liver a burden. Because the lungs
are easiest to lift from the body,
they were called the lights.
Now that they've taken one from you
you're lighter still
and your voice thinner
as though you would talk like some noise
through the trees.
One breath keeps you drifting
away from us and the ground
as we jump up to pull you down
and secure you to the visible world.

Meanwhile the Elephants

Watching this orchestra wield its instruments,
I wonder how many blind people it takes
to describe the elephant. Not that these musicians—
serious as pallbearers and waiters—are no good
at interpreting the score, but ninety-eight
men and women working their bows, shutting down
the valves in gentle fury, they seem trying
to understand a beast together, to map
its proportions, to add, divide and measure it
with brassy canes, with varnished paddles. But they don't
finish even as they finish, the last strings
patted and shushed up.

                    If you put a blind person
at every inch of the beast and they touched
it all over, its folds and faults, pointillists
at a canvas, an orchestra crammed in a closet,
could they, in the end—together—abstract
the elephant the way science abstracts the frozen
distances between stars? Or would they need to fell
the beast to know it, unwind its entrails like points
of logic? Even then, as they lifted the heart,
big as a French horn, the smell of blood
strong as a single idea in their heads,
would they understand that this chambered
and valved instrument irrigated the dead land
piled at their knees? And the little guy who gets lost
in the cavity and wanders like a wise fetus,
does he know more, or less, than the others?

Meanwhile the elephants trumpet through the trees.
They are so huge even when they run
they must keep two feet on the ground
at all times. They cannot jump.
They plow into muddy pools, suck water up,
and throw a lake over their shoulders.
The shore shakes like an old rug: the blind
hear thunder in the crushed jungle. Run for cover.

Sestina to Stanley Fish

Propped up in bed to read, the humid
night pressing against the screens, your reader
makes the meaning out of the text,
a rickety kite tied to the thumb.
The author begins with few words, a tap on the shoulder
that says, "Let me tell you a story."

But your reader argues, "I'm the one telling the story:
The night a plumped pillow, the air humid—"
Skimming the page, a fly shoulders
the thick air, becomes loose punctuation the reader
claps in his book. His pinched thumb
holds his place, but he's lost track of the text.

Though if he makes it, how can he lose the text?
Like yeast, his mind lifts the flat story
into meaning, leaving his mark like a thumb
pressed into dough. He backs up: "The air humid,
pressing, my mother hummed in her kitchen"—the reader
wanders off again—"her rickety shoulders

tensing as the iron steamed into a shirt's shoulder."
Surely he's lost his place now. Or found another text?
one monogrammed like the cuff links the reader
sees shining from his dresser, two more eyes on his story:
"Roped up in bed, to read the human
night, I must compress the dream tied to my thumb,

ignore what tugs like sorrow from the other end, the thumping
in the casements."—He's been drinking tonight—"I shudder
as the wind picks up amid the humble
rickety houses, hums through crawl spaces, and tests
joints time has loosened: My mother is dying. I'm sorry
I paid no mind till now. Crossing the stubble, the reaper—"

Downstairs on its spindly stand, the telephone reports
a late alarm. The hospital? His heart pumps
in his hands. He lays the book down, glances at the starry
night. Lone headlights, cottages closed and shuttered.
My god, he realizes, it's winter. The story teased
him into summer, shut out the dry textures of hunger. . . .

The author goes on writing over the reader's shoulder—
while you thumb on through the text—closing
his mother's story, thin breath lost to the humid room.

Inward, from the Air

(R. M. 1953-1979)

to leaf tip, then stem, pith, xylem, to zygote,
to carbon and further to the very atoms,
or musing in the reverse . . .

But there's always the lawnmower next door,
a dog at the end of its chain like a compass point.
The past had its own distractions—the call

from the lettuce wagon, shouts of a crowd
at the far end of the square, teasing
the riot into the noise of a festival.

The things of this world offer too much.
Cream in glazed bowls, misted
blueberries, and the affectionate

hand on my shoulder—all simultaneous
with her on the dark street
the last time I saw her, one side of her face lit

by a shop window, the other toward me.
We had nothing much to talk about.
A man who loved me waited in the idling car.

Later I complained she was too lively
to be dead so easily, laid out serene
in the pose that tells our weakness:

as though she were listening intently
to herself. If I could cancel out
these soothing distractions, the light falling

on the patched walk, what then?
Risk the irreversible vision? exiled
like the astronaut cut off and drifting

through silence above the blue
and green world. Yet even the mad
sometimes hear the scraping

feet of attendants. But she—
in that sealed auditorium, the blank screen—
her concentration is perfect.

Tennyson Under the Yews

How much it must have hurt him
to imagine the embrace, the roots cocooning
the body of his dead friend Hallam,
adopting his shape as we might
the gestures of a friend, spilling in
where the flesh fell away like sand-
castle turrets melting with the tide.
In this way the second violinist picks up the note
when the first has slumped forward,
cradling the fiddle, as if that would help,
and the orchestra never misses the beat
his heart does. The world allows no empty spaces—
the myths tell us. For every old man
who drops his hoe and sinks
into his garden, there is the infant
incandescent in the clouds, waiting
to take on the bright skins
of richly beating blood. The leaves settle
and the snows cover them or the wind
carries them along the fence while the trees
fill up with buds, small scars.
Not that there's no sympathy. Look at the stories:
grandmother's clock—to the very minute—
it stopped when she did, the delicate weights
that dangled in its case could never be righted.
And the one about the violinist, every string
broke with his passing and the violin
resisted the music of all other fingers.
And Tennyson under the yews, coming back
each spring when their pollen lifted off
and drifted as a living smoke
over Hallam's grave. Imagine him listening
as the tendrils felt their way along,
trying on the rings, plucking the tendons,
and knocking the buttons into dull music.

November 1917

I won't lie to you.
They are nothing to me, these two men
lying wounded in the mud at Passchendaele.
And even if they went back to the slop
of the trenches, and managed to live the last year
of the war, they'd hardly be alive
70 years later to be more than mist
in trousers and coat, a few pennies in a pocket—
and how could I find out from that
how they got along later,
if the world drifted back into place
like streamers down from balconies
and the drums fading with morning?
So you see, there's no reason to trouble them
into recollection. The alphabet of their bodies
gives us ample characters to shape a plot—
though, of course, we are to them
just faces in pine cones, the frothy clothes
the sea piles on the rocks.
Their faces are indistinct.
We could fit our own faces into them
as into the cardboard people at carnivals.
When we say time stops,
don't we mean it stops being important,
experience sharpened to a pencil point
to stab at one moment? From this alphabet
we read how nothing now matters to them
but the craving satisfied. One must be the other's prisoner,
but they have forgotten which.
The wounded Canadian leans up on his left elbow,
like someone lying before a mirror:
the wounded German leans on his right
to suck a light from the cigarette held out
in the mouth of the enemy, close enough to kiss,
too close to afford self-consciousness,
or the photographer's hard irony.
How evenly our side looks into theirs,

his eyes waiting for the other to look up,
signaling that the fire has taken hold
and they can break apart and lie back in the field
that has smeared their hearts like cabbages.

Hook and Ladder

A smoking mattress dragged across the porch,
then sodden, smoking clothes—the fire fighters
carry them out like punished cats and dump them

on the too-green grass. The long blue robe rounds
his house again (three times now, I've watched him)
into a gust of wind that exposes

his white hairy legs. He had no time to dress.
A few neighbors stand sipping from cups they carried
from their breakfast tables. He circles

his house again. What can he do but watch?
His life heaped in dirty measure at the curb.
The men bring down their picks, thwacking the roof

shingles like grey egg shell. The smoke explodes
from the attic and shoves us back as if we'd
kept it cooped up all morning. Our eyes sting

but we keep watching, the private made public,
its damaged emblems burning on the lawn. The man
in his old robe is so stunned he doesn't see

his indiscretion, on display like lovers
fighting at a picnic grounds, that old man
yesterday sobbing in the soup aisle.

The way we shift each other from eye to eye
like truants at a lecture, the way we all
go back to our houses and click the doors

shut although it's nearing 90—I think
of how much we depend on ignorance,
how we choose it, how we need to choose it

as if one's life story were a rickety
sky that can hold up one star at a time.
Too many novas on that thin roof and we might

break through. It's the decent thing to do—
isn't it? Offer sympathy, prayers quick
as smoke signals and hope his roof can hold him?

The Night of the Breaking Glass

A windshield crazy with breaks
like a skating rink deserted. The young
run random in the street. Upstairs, their families.
The drawn shades throb with the lights
from a squad car burning quietly below.
The cops hustle by in pairs,
wide-eyed, jangling with equipment. Invisible
as a loose page blown against door frames and worried
about the road, my father, the newsman, reels
into the summer of 1967, the race riot.
He's either drunk
or out of his mind—that delicate organ
misfiring, a gun carried
in the hat. He could find *the story of his life*
among the shards and blackened TV sets
and relay lines passing hand to hand
the wealth of a state store. He lived here once,
maybe that's why he shows up on this street
stumbling. He's lost his childhood
or found it
when he falls into the park, into the custody
of a juniper that keeps him,
as I would, for the night.

The moment a window shatters it looks like a pond
stirred up by a wishing coin
or a dropped body. And the faces,
losing their reflections in the rocking water,
could be breaking in grief
or in laughter. The viewer chooses
since the facts are indifferent.
When we make stories out of appearances
we almost control the world
that always controls us. The bicycle rusting
in the city dump, its one wheel
spinning with the breeze, we squint
until it's a baby's mobile. Or a cattle car
speeding into Poland.

Kristallnacht, 1938, an old Jew behind the curtains
looks down the street to the riot.
His shop will go soon, bricks raining
the glass across the checkered floor,
knocking over bolts of chenille and jersey,
he thinks, like wooden soldiers. The flames will race
up the sheer marquisette
he draped along the counter as down a road
that never ends since he never began it.
Shoe buckles will melt into black felt, going soft
like faces in old lithographs: with the jawbone
of an ass Samson scattered the Philistines.
But the old man reaches for his own face,
feeling for the bones that rise
more each year—the stones of a dying stream
whose town empties so quickly.

By the time they round the corner, he's changed
the brown shirts into loosed dam water
bobbing with torches. And he's prepared
for each glass bead that dissolves
like the sledding snows of his childhood.

My father rouses himself, hat in the grass, one leg
looped over a branch
as if it belonged to someone else.
Whatever story he made, to explain himself
to himself, out of the park trash
and his coat sleeve—torn off and folded
into his breast pocket—
he couldn't tell his children
since he didn't know where he'd been
and the tale reached us
with another meaning entirely.

Gladiolus

for a child who was never born

Where my life would have gone with you
is not as bad as I imagined:
stuck somewhere like Sulphur Springs, Ohio,
you thrashing in a grubby bassinet,
workweeks dropped like blank pie
from an office clock, weekends dragged
from an in-law's speed boat, lake water
like the green glass of a wine bottle
with me inside, a genie no incantation
could force out. Nor would it have gone

as easily as here in my 32nd year,
settling papery bulbs into silky pockets.
All day I need answer no one, so my thoughts
can spill quick as water from a rain spout
and fan out across last fall's leaves.
Now that you're old enough to listen,
now that you've come to that age
you would have been,
now that the soil has burned off the frost's glitter
and rustles beneath my fingers,

I see how you have grown impatient for me.
It used to sicken me, earthworms uncoiling
from the roots of wild onion, the anarchy
of pill bugs beneath a fallen branch.
But smeared and shining to my elbows with mud,
the hand aching that held the claw,
I see now where you have gone to wait for me.
With canteen and rope I'm outfitting myself,
I'm coming down to get you, to bring you back
in crimson trumpets dense along the pliant spear.

C O L O P H O N

This book is set in the Merganthaler version of Palatino, a
typeface aptly named for the Italian scribe because of its
calligraphic strokes. It is printed on Glatfelter acid-free paper.
The design is by Gary Gore. Cover design by Stella Bonds.